HAMLET
AND THE ENORMOUS CHINESE DRAGON KITE

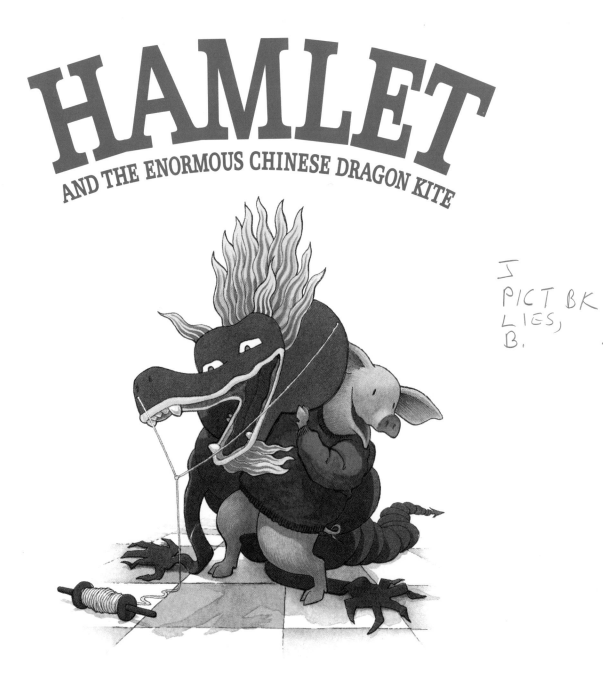

BRIAN LIES

Houghton Mifflin Company
Boston 1994

Library of Congress Cataloging-in-Publication Data

Lies, Brian.
    Hamlet and the enormous Chinese dragon kite / Brian Lies.
        p.   cm.
    Summary: Despite the worries of his porcupine friend Quince,
Hamlet the pig tries flying an enormous red dragon kite and has an
aerial adventure.
    ISBN 0-395-68391-2
    [1. Kites—Fiction.   2. Pigs—Fiction.   3. Porcupines—Fiction.]
        I. Title.
PZ7.L618Ham   1994   93-30726
[E]—dc20   CIP
                            AC

Printed in the United States of America

WOZ   10   9   8   7   6   5   4   3   2   1

For my grandmothers,
Bertha Sherwood Bonham and
Josephine Bollman Lies

HAMLET sat on his thinking rock at the top of Hamlet's Hill and watched as crisp fall leaves blew by.

Quince paced back and forth with a worried expression on his face. But that wasn't new. Quince was always worried about *something*.

"Quince," Hamlet announced, "I've made a decision."

"Oh, no!" Quince squeaked, pacing faster. "Not again! Whenever you say that, I get a bad feeling. Remember the time you decided to go rock climbing? I warned you not to do it. Remember when you tried painting? They still haven't fixed the town clock. And I warned you not to take swimming lessons, either. But you didn't listen, and you know what happened."

"Yes, yes, I remember," Hamlet admitted, "but this is different. This time nothing can happen. I'm going to get a kite."

"A kite!" Quince gasped. "They're dangerous! You'll get string burn!"

Hamlet laughed and started down the path to the village.

"You're such a worrier," he told Quince, who jounced along behind him, squeaking protests. "I'm not talking about white-water rafting, or bullfighting, or anything like that. I'm going to get a *kite*, for heaven's sake."

"People who fly kites always get string burn. Or—or they get carried off!" Quince insisted, waving his paws. "You'll never catch *me* flying a kite. No, sir. It's a bad idea, Hamlet."

Hamlet's mind was on the kite he'd seen in the general store. It looked like a fierce, red Chinese dragon with big claws and a long, winding tail. He could just imagine how it would look swooping through the air at the end of a string—*his* string.

"Yes, it's a perfect day for flying a kite," he declared.

When Hamlet opened the door of the general store, a bell jangled somewhere far inside. He headed straight for the kites, with Quince in tow.

"See? Isn't it *great?*" Hamlet asked, holding up the dragon kite.

Quince's jaw dropped and his quills stood up straight. "Not that one! What if there's a knight lurking in the woods and while you're carrying it home, he mistakes you for a dragon? Knights carry sharp swords, you know."

Quince held up another kite. It was tiny and squarish and the color of cold oatmeal. "How about this one? This one looks safe."

Hamlet wrinkled his nose. It was ugly. Nothing at all like the beautiful Chinese dragon kite with the fierce claws and long, winding tail. Now *that* was a kite!

Hamlet went to pay for the kite and the shopkeeper raised his eyebrows. "Kind of a big kite for such a small pig," he remarked. "Perhaps one of the smaller dragons might be better."

Quince nodded. He poked Hamlet. "See? He thinks so too. Oh, there's going to be trouble! Mark my words!" He waved the tiny, oatmeal-colored kite. "If you absolutely *have* to get a kite, get this one!"

Hamlet shook his head. His mind was made up.

Hamlet gathered the dragon kite in his arms and headed home. Quince followed, muttering in his tiny voice, "Trouble's coming! Just you wait and see. And don't come crying to me when you get carried away. Just you remember I told you so."

Hamlet took the kite to the field near his house, where the wind was strong. He let out some string, walked back a few steps, and tugged gently. Quince started pacing.

The wind caught hold of the kite, and it soared up into the sky with a *whoosh*. It danced and dodged and looped around like a real dragon. Soon the enormous kite was just a tiny red squiggle in the sky.

Hamlet felt wonderful. This was the life—a swift breeze, an enormous kite, and an endless blue sky to sail it in . . .

Then the kite gave a strong jolt. Hamlet had come to the end of the string and the kite was tugging harder and harder. He leaned way back, but the kite pulled him upright again.

"Oh, help!" Quince cried. "Fire! Flood! Disaster! Let go of the kite, Hamlet! It's too windy! Let go!"

That was the most ridiculous thing Hamlet had ever heard. Let go of the beautiful Chinese dragon kite? Never.

Then the kite gave another enormous yank. Hamlet flew completely off his feet and sailed toward the trees at the other end of the field.

Quince ran along beneath Hamlet, yelling, "Let go, Hamlet! Jump! Jump, and I'll catch you!"

Hamlet eyed Quince's sharp quills. That didn't seem like a good idea. Besides, if he let go of the kite, he would lose it forever. So he hung on.

The kite lifted him higher and higher. His feet scraped the tops of trees as he passed over them. The farther up he went, the worse the idea of letting go seemed. Hamlet could still hear Quince's tiny voice shouting up at him.

"I knew it!" it squeaked. "I knew it! I knew no good would come of this! Oh, help! Fire! Flood! Disaster! Oh, help!" But soon Quince's cries were gone, carried off by the wind.

Hamlet began to enjoy the flight, now that he was away from Quince and all his worries. He could see the whole village from up here, and the next village over, and even the village beyond that. "This is what birds see," he marveled. "I'm free! It feels wonderful to fly! Quince is silly to worry about something as wonderful as this!"

"Beautiful day," Hamlet remarked to an eagle, who was so startled to see him that she dropped the fish she was carrying home to the eaglets in her nest.

"A flying pig?" she cried. Then she glanced up and saw the dragon kite far above him. "Oh! I see." She nodded, with big eyes. "That dragon is kidnapping you? Well, don't you worry. We'll fix it!"

"No, I'm just flying a kite," Hamlet protested, but the eagle was already gone and didn't hear him.

Hamlet wondered what she meant by fixing it.

"I hope this wind dies down soon," he thought, watching the ground rush by far below him. "I don't know how much longer I can hang on." He was starting to wish he had let go of the kite when Quince first suggested it.

Then the kite string made a loud noise.

Twannng!

To his horror, Hamlet saw a whole swarm of eagles high above him attacking his beautiful kite. He yelled up at them, "Stop! It's only a kite, not a real dragon! Everything is all right! *Please* leave it alone!"

But the eagles were so far away they could barely hear him.
They dived at the kite, tore it with their beaks, and shredded the paper
with their sharp claws—and Hamlet started to drop.

The eagles thought the dragon was trying to get away, and so they attacked it faster and harder, ripping and tearing until there wasn't anything left but broken sticks, some string, and a blizzard of red paper.

Hamlet fell faster and faster.

"Help!" he shouted. "Help me! I'm falling!"

But the eagles thought he was thanking them. They waved to him happily and swooped away home to brag about their bravery.

The ground zoomed up toward Hamlet, but he smiled at his good luck. "I'm headed straight for that pond." He grinned. "A nice, soft landing!"

The pond grew bigger and bigger as he sped toward it.

"Now I'm glad I took those swimming lessons, even though Quince said I'd get swimmer's ear or turn all wrinkly. For once I can tell *him* 'I told you so.'"

Hamlet missed the pond.

But fortunately the kite string snarled in the branches of a gigantic tree.

Hamlet found himself hanging upside down from one of the largest branches, tangled in the remains of the Chinese dragon kite. Once it had fierce claws and a long, winding tail. Now it looked like a pile of sticks.

"It's not funny," he told the cows who were resting in the shade under the maple tree. "I'm stuck! Would somebody please help me down from here?"

The cows nibbled at the kite string until Hamlet fell with a *kerthump* on the ground.

"There. That's much better," one of the cows said, as Hamlet dusted himself off and made sure no bones were broken.

One of the other cows shook her head and scolded him, "You really shouldn't be flying in the first place, you know. You don't have the wings for it."

"I *know* that," Hamlet groaned. It was no fun to be criticized while sitting in the wreckage of his beautiful kite.

He gathered the remains of the kite under one arm, thanked the cows, and trudged homeward. It was a long, dusty walk, and it was starting to get cold.

Quince hurried out to meet Hamlet as he walked up Hamlet's Hill. "There you are! You have no idea how worried I've been! Are you hurt? Do you have string burn?" Hamlet shook his head, and Quince took the shredded remains of the glorious Chinese dragon kite from him. He set them gently on the rubbish heap behind the house.

"I made some hot chocolate," Quince said. "I hope you don't mind me using your kitchen, but I know how much you like hot chocolate after one of your adventures. And I even got whipped cream," he added.

Hamlet collapsed into his favorite chair and sighed as Quince handed him a steaming cup piled high with whipped cream. *What else does a pig need*, Hamlet thought, *besides solid ground under his feet, a cup of hot chocolate, and a good friend?*

Unless . . .

He'd just had a brilliant idea.